Fossil Fuels

Julie Haydon

CONTENTS

NELSON
CENGAGE Learning

Australia • Brazil • Japan • Korea • Mexico • Singapore • Spain • United Kingdom • United States

Fuel

Fuel is anything that is burned to make heat or power.

A **power station** burns fuel to make electricity.

A car burns fuel
to make its engine go.

A gas stove burns fuel
to make heat.

oil

coal

Fossil Fuels

Coal, oil and natural gas are fuels.
These fuels are used a lot today.

coal

natural gas

oil

Coal, oil and natural gas
are found in the earth's crust.
They are called fossil fuels.

How Did Fossil Fuels

Fossil fuels began to form
millions of years ago.
They formed from
dead plants and animals.

The dead plants
and animals were
under layers
of mud and sand

Form?

fossil fuels

buried

Over a long time,
the dead plants and animals
changed into fossil fuels.

Coal

Coal is black or brown rock.

People have used coal for fuel
for thousands of years.

Long ago, coal was dug out
of the ground with simple hand tools.

Today, miners use
big machines
to cut or scoop
coal from mines.

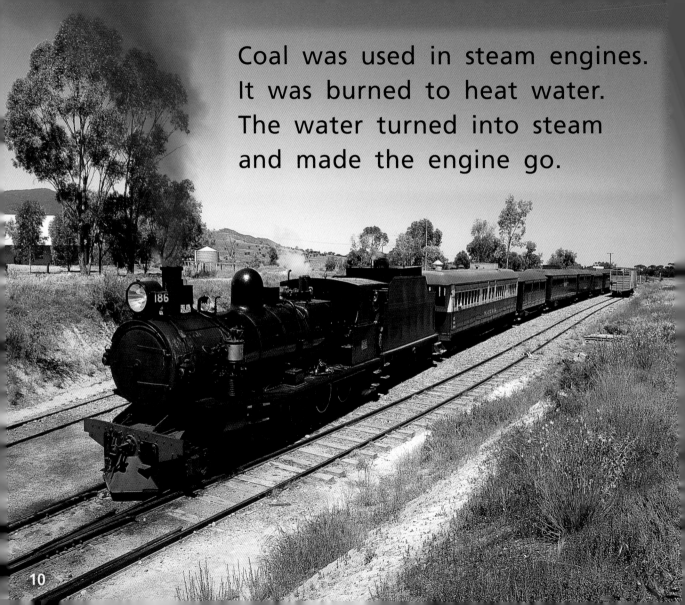

Coal was used in steam engines.
It was burned to heat water.
The water turned into steam
and made the engine go.

Today, coal is burned in power stations to make electricity.

Electricity powers our homes, offices and factories.

Oil and Natural Gas

Oil is a thick, black liquid.

Natural gas is a gas that you cannot see.

Oil and natural gas are found
deep under the ground
or under the sea.

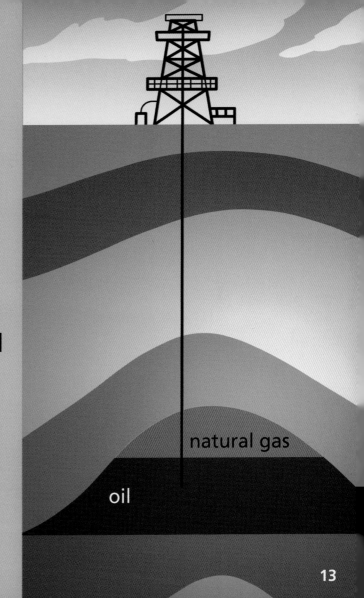

natural gas

oil

People drill wells to reach oil or natural gas.

First, **rigs** are built.
The tall tower on a rig has a big drill.
The drill cuts through soil, sand and rock.

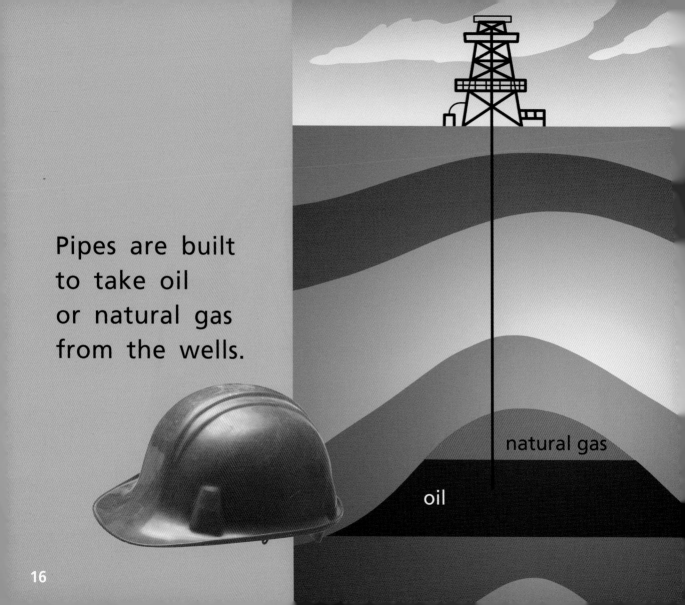

Pipes are built
to take oil
or natural gas
from the wells.

natural gas

oil

16

Sometimes, oil is drilled
from under the sea floor.
Ships take it back to land.

On land, oil is pumped to an oil **refinery**. The oil travels through pipes.

At the refinery, the oil
is made into many things.

On land, natural gas travels through pipes to a gas **plant**. At the plant, the natural gas is made ready for use.

Natural gas goes to homes,
offices and factories
through pipes under the ground.

Fossil Fuels and the Future

One day, the earth will run out of fossil fuels.
People have started using **solar** energy and wind energy instead of fossil fuels.

wind energy

solar energy

Glossary

plant a place like a factory. Natural gas goes to a gas plant.

power station a place where electricity is made

refinery a factory where things, like oil, are changed into goods

rigs towers built above oil or gas wells

solar of the sun

Index